Mouth Almighty

A play
by Salihah Agbaje

Acknowledgements

All thanks and praise is due to the Almighty and Most Merciful. I will never be able to explain my gratitude for this opportunity or any other that You have offered me. Please accept my thanks and continue to be my Guide, amen.

I would like to acknowledge the help given to me by the special men in my life, my sons; Sugar Daddy Number 1 & Sugar Daddy Number 2 ☺, the lights of my life! I pray you both appreciate this end product when you are old enough; thank you for your patience.

B, thank you for reminding me of my primary objective whenever it got surrounded by various distractions. Your guiding hand, love and assistance in compiling the manuscript in its various stages, enabled me to bring this book to completion!

How can I ever fully express how blessed I am to have such lovely siblings! I am so glad I can call on you any time of the day or night to receive your calming and wise counsel.

T, what would I do without your ever ready alternative ideas? You are a wealth of knowledge for me to continuously tap into and you never complain when I go off on a tangent!

You have travelled along this eventful journey with me and I thank you from the bottom of my heart for all your patience, assistance and undying encouragement to get the job done!

O, thank you for listening so well to my ideas as they evolved and laughing alongside me as I made silly mistakes and lived to tell the tale. I am grateful for your assistance and advice on the serious matters.

Toy, my other half ☺ You have smiled and sighed with me, moaned and shouted with me and now you can breathe a sigh of relief with me! Thank you for your encouragement and belief and for being there for me. Thank you for being so passionate about *Mouth Almighty.*

Mum, Bro, thanks for your prayers and support. Special thanks to Rafiq and Yasmeen (my research team) who offered limitless, up-to-date information to help keep the characters as authentic as possible.

An extra special mention to Naberay Paul-Wright for reading and reviewing the drafts and being a genuine driving force when I started to slow down. Uncle L, thanks for all of your assistance and technical support, I appreciate the time you gave. Nikki Reynolds, a true inspiration! Thank you for 'living' *Mouth Almighty* alongside me over the summer, you're a star! I love you all mucho!

My thanks also to Yemi Akinsiwaju, for your speedy and thorough editorial assistance in making the final draft a more polished product and my very talented artist, Waheed Akhtar, responsible for the book cover and character illustrations. My gratitude to you both.

Finally my thanks goes to those that have played any part in reading, listening, talking about or contributing in any way to the creation of the finished product of *Mouth Almighty.* It is my hope that the messages within the play are carried far and wide among people of all walks of life but specifically our youth. I agree fully with those that say it takes a whole village to raise a child and hope that I am making a valid contribution to raising our children positively through this book.

Table of Contents

Cast of Characters			6
Key Characters			7
Act 1	Scene 1	Close Your Mouth!	9
	Scene 2	Follow Me	11
Act 2	Scene 1	Looking For My Best Friend	15
	Scene 2	If You Want A Job Done Properly	18
	Scene 3	Will The Real Mr Cringe Please Stand Up?	23
	Scene 4	Desperate Measures	26
Act 3	Scene 1	What's That Noise?	29
	Scene 2	Looking For Justice	30
	Scene 3	Call In The Professionals	31
	Scene 4	Meet The Dwarves	34
Act 4	Scene 1	Safe But Not Quite Sound	38
	Scene 2	The Singing Villain	39
Act 5	Scene 1	Hold The Fort Tata!	42
	Scene 2	Bud Among The Taste Buds	44
	Scene 3	Justice Comes Clean	50
	Scene 4	By George, Fancy That!	73
Act 6	Scene 1	Another Unsuspecting Individual	77
	Scene 2	Back To Being The Sidekick	79
	Scene 3	Seek And You Shall Find	85
	Scene 4	Strike Two	86
	Scene 5	The Police Station	88
	Scene 6	Typical!	90
Act 7	Scene 1	The Crazy Scientist Strikes Again	91
	Scene 2	Busted!	96
Appendices			110
Music Scores			111
About The Author			143

Cast of Characters

Justice
Hope
Emmanuel
Tata
Faith
Wallace
Chico
Mr Cringe
Bud
The Choir
George
Mrs Alexander
Marcus
Marcus' Sidekick
Police Constable
Police Constable 1
Police Constable 2
Police Constable 3
Receptionist
Nurse
Team Of Armed Police Officers
Silent Strangers (Extras)

Key Characters

Justice	A tall 11 year old boy with a bold personality. He is dressed in school uniform for most of the play
Hope	Justice's mother is a hardworking and somewhat bitter woman that is tired of her marriage. She has an exhausted look about her
Emmanuel	Justice's father is grubby in appearance and is often fixed to the living room arm chair when not at the book makers. He's a good man but a little lazy!
Tata	Tata is Justice's best friend, he is slightly shorter than Justice and wears glasses. He also wears school uniform but looks much tidier than Justice
Faith	Tata's mother is very conservative and dresses in a smart and formal fashion
Wallace	Tata's father is a very hands-on dad and a good husband. He is the opposite of Emmanuel
Mr Cringe	A tall man with a dark demeanour and a sinister look about him. He can be played as a slightly older gentleman, slightly hunched over or middle aged with a strong stature but always smartly dressed
Bud	A little person dressed in overalls and a cap. A very cheerful individual representing 'The Choir'

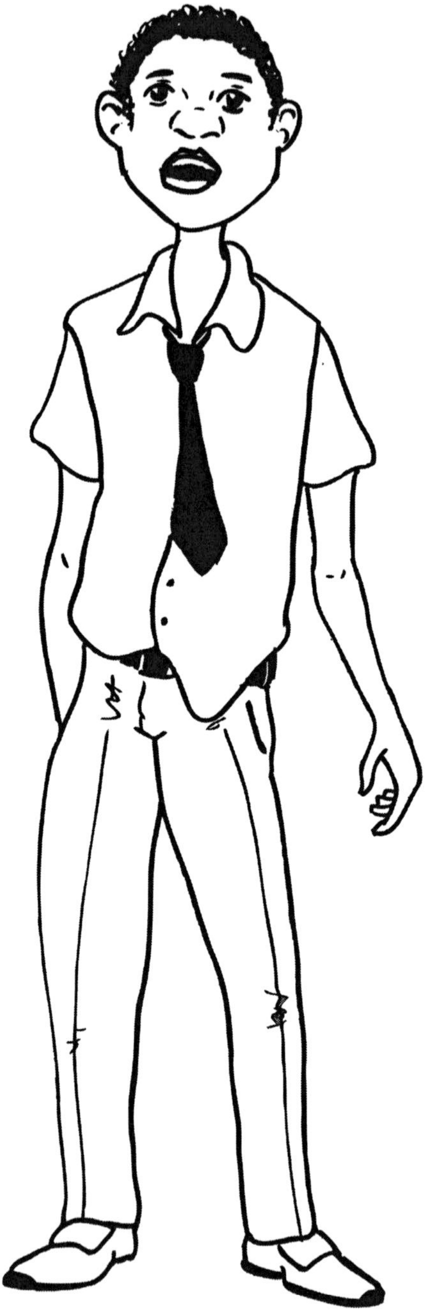

Justice

Act 1, Scene 1

Close Your Mouth!

At Justice's house, in the kitchen: it's a modest and very basic room and, although it is stark, it is clean.

Justice: Muuuuuuuuum?

Hope: Yes, Justice? What is it?

Justice: What you doing?

Hope: You can see that I'm cooking.

Justice: What you cooking?

Hope: Dinner!

Justice: So, what's for dinner?

Hope: You, if you're not careful! What's the matter? Don't you have homework to do?

Justice gets closer to where his mum is standing, stirring something in a large pot on the stove.

Justice: Done already!

Hope: Really! Well, take it to your dad to check it, please. *(She raises her voice so that it can be heard in the adjacent room)* That's if he can be bothered at all! If it's not too much trouble for him! But before you do that, run to the shop and buy me a pint of milk.

Justice: OK, mum.

Hope: And Justice?

Justice: Yes, mum?

Hope: Close your mouth! I don't know how many times a day I have to say it. Keep your mouth closed! It's a terrible habit you've got. You'll see what happens if you don't give it up. Now go straight to the shop and come straight back ... don't even think about going to Tata's house or anywhere else for that matter. Is that clear?

Justice: Yes, mum.

Exit Justice. Justice collects some money from his mum and puts his coat on. He exits his house and slowly makes his way across the road.

Tata's house is very near and the temptation to go over and throw a stone at Tata's bedroom window is almost too much to resist, but resist he does! Instead, he focuses on putting one foot in front of the other and sings to his pace.

Act 1, Scene 2

Follow Me

Outside Justice's house: Justice walks towards the local shop. The street is fairly empty, he breaks into song.

Song: *Justice Is My Name*

> Justice is my name and excitement is my game,
> Wherever boredom goes, I won't follow!
> You can take away my sidekick and my favourite game,
> I'll be having fun all the same.
>
> As far as it goes, it's difficult to see
> Me in the same place as boredom may ever be
> I am always at the end where fun is running mad,
> With Tata and me around, you'll only ever be glad!
>
> Yeah, Justice is my name, fun is the only game…(repeat)

Justice makes his way down the road and across the zebra crossing, but he is so caught up in his song that he doesn't realise that the peculiar-looking old man that was leaning against a wall, cleaning his fingernails with a pocket knife, is now following closely behind.

Mr Cringe: Justice? Is that your name?

Justice: Yeah.

Mr Cringe: What a strange name for a child!

Justice doesn't know how to take this and just gawps at the strange man with his mouth open.

Mr Cringe: What a large mouth you have! It's almost big enough to fit both my fists inside!

Justice: No it's not! I may have a big mouth but it's not as big as your head!

Mr Cringe: Ho ho hah! Well, you really do have a big mouth, don't you, boy? I admire your guts, talking back like that. You can't know who I am. You don't, do you?

Justice: No. Who are you?

Mr Cringe: Do you believe in magic, boy?

With a flourish, Mr Cringe produces a bouquet of flowers from his sleeve. Justice snorts, unimpressed. But with another flourish, Mr Cringe waves his hand over the flowers and they impressively morph into a writhing snake.

Justice gasps and his mouth inevitably drops open. Mr Cringe notes the impression he has made and feels satisfied. He blows dramatically over the snake and it turns into a stick of rock.

Mr Cringe: Some say I'm a magician, some say I'm a weirdo, but I would say I'm an opportunistic businessman!

Song: *Follow Me*

Well the wonderful thing about me you see
Is all the versatility,
I offer this and I offer that,
I've more than two feathers in me cap!

Hocus pocus and zippadidoo,
I'm something different, something new,
I'm something rare and don't you know,
This magic stuff is not for show!
It's real you see and whatsmore,
I'm sure of how to double the score.
Bringing fun and joy around
When boredom was all that could be found.

Chorus:
Yes, the wonderful thing about me you see
Is all the versatility,
I offer this and offer that,
I've more than two or three feathers in me cap!

Magical worlds are in my hands,
Come close my boy,
And I'll show you lands,
Beyond your wildest dreams and more
This kind of stuff you've not seen before!

At this stage, Mr Cringe produces illusion upon illusion, created by lights and graphics for stage.

Repeat Chorus

Justice, what's your desire?
Money? Fame? Climbing higher?
I can make your life more interesting shall we say?
Follow me to somewhere more private and we'll play.
Are you ready to experience something new and surreal?
You'll only get this one chance so don't go and blow it,
how do you feel?
How do you feel?
After some excitement?
After something new?
Well come on then, boy
You know what to do!
Let's have some fun, follow me, come along
Enjoying yourself just can't be wrong.

Chorus x 2

At this stage, Justice is singing along in the chorus and is enthralled by the song and dance. He has cast aside any worries or concerns he had about this strange-looking man and is ready to follow his new friend along a path of mystery. Milk for his mother is but a very distant memory, as is his old sidekick, Tata.

Act 2, Scene 1

Looking for My Best Friend

At Tata's house, in his bedroom. His house and particularly his bedroom are more modern and look far more expensive than Justice's. The bedroom is comfortable and cosy, with all the typical mod cons.

Tata is bored and with very little to do, he prepares to take a nap. Although he's not tired, he knows the boredom will bring sleep. Offstage the phone rings, but Tata doesn't move. He hears his dad call to him but he still doesn't move. He hears footsteps. It's one of his brothers.

Chico: Oi, big head! Dad's calling you. Like you never heard!

Tata: I never heard!

Chico: Yeah, right! Get off your butt and stop crying for your boyfriend!

Justice is bad news anyway, the big-mouth freak!

Tata: Oh shut up! He's not my boyfriend! What you talking about? Just 'cause you don't have any friends!

Chico slams the door as he laughs loudly at his own joke. Tata slowly drags himself downstairs to where his parents are standing next to the telephone.

Faith: Tata, have you heard from Justice at all? Think before you answer.

Tata: No, mama.

Wallace: Are you sure? We've just had his mother on the phone. She's looking for him. She says she sent him for milk hours ago and he hasn't come home.

Tata: Well, I haven't seen him.

Faith: Has he called you? This is serious, you know? Where's your mobile?

Tata: Upstairs.

Wallace: Has he called?

Tata: Errr, nope.

Faith: Go and get it; you don't sound sure.

Tata exits reluctantly.

Wallace: What do you think?

Faith: Not sure. Those two are always up to something, but Justice is always the ringleader; he's got a big mouth, I mean figuratively as well as literally. He's off the rails that boy. I don't want him leading Tata astray.

Wallace: Well, we've separated them and I don't believe Tata has seen him. He knows what he'll get if he does!

Enter Tata with a modest looking mobile phone.

Tata: Here it is.

His mother reaches for it and examines it.

Faith: OK. Well, I'll hold on to it for now, just in case.

(Tata huffs loudly)

Wallace: I heard that. You're still on a warning because of your antics at school, so don't let me deal with you right now. Out!

Exit Tata.

Act 2, Scene 2

If You Want A Job Done Properly

At Justice's house: his mum is wondering where her son has got to ... SFX: the loud sound of a clock ticking echoes in the background. She's pacing the front room whilst Justice's father pulls off his boots. It's been over three hours and there is no sign of Justice yet.

Hope: What did the man at the corner shop say? Did he see Justice?

Emmanuel: Nope. There's been no sign of him all day.

Hope: So, where else did you try?

Emmanuel: Ummmm. Well, I thought he'd be back by now.

Hope: What! So you walked to the shop and back without even searching the area? Just typical of you.
Can't you do anything properly? How could you do that? He's missing.
He's never been gone like this before; the shop is three minutes away and my boy's been gone over three hours.
I knew I couldn't rely on you.
Don't you care at all?

Hope is so irate at this stage. She begins to locate her shoes.

Emmanuel: What? Stop over-reacting. He'll be making his way back now.

Hope: How do you know? He could be laying in a ditch anywhere, God forbid!
What's wrong with you? Your child is missing!
Is it too much to expect you to look for him? Oh, why do I bother?

Emmanuel: As usual, you're over-reacting.
What's this all about? No, don't bother.
I can see what this is about.

Hope: What? What is it about?

Emmanuel: Last night.

Hope: Last night? Are you so self absorbed that you really think I'm still talking about that?
I can't be bothered to keep going on about you sitting in the bookies or the pub or wherever else you'd rather be when you could be working or even looking for work. I mean, when was the last time you applied for a job?
Any kind of job? What about that advert for a porter in the paper shop window?

Emmanuel: What about it?

Hope: Did you apply for it? I already know the answer to that.

Emmanuel: Hope. I am an educated man! Do you expect me to be somebody's dog's body?

Hope: I expect you to be a man! Is it too much for you to bring money into the house as opposed to gambling it away?
Emmanuel, you should be looking for Justice, that's what this is about.
But you can't see that, can you?
I'll tell you what else you can't see. Justice, and the way he looks at you.

Emmanuel: Oh and what's that supposed to mean?

Hope: He sees you as a disappointment. You're never home, you don't partake in his life and you have nothing to offer him – or me for that matter!

Emmanuel: I'm around plenty!

Hope: I can't deal with this. I should have known better than to believe in you, I've got to find my son.

She begins to pull on her jacket.

I told him to come straight home.
I thought I could trust him to do such a small thing without going missing. Where is he?
What if something has happened to him?

Emmanuel: Nothing's happened to him. You know what Justice is like; he's probably hiding out in Tata's house.

Hope: I told you, I called Tata's mother already and they've not seen Justice.
I've got no idea where else he could be and it's been over three hours already. I've got to find him.

Emmanuel: No. I'll go again. He may come home before I find him, so just stay here.
I'll be back as soon as I can be and I've got my phone on me; try not to worry.

Hope: And where are you going to look?
You've got no idea, so what's the point?

She attempts to move to the door again, but Emmanuel blocks her way.

Emmanuel: Just stay here. I will find him!

Exit Emmanuel. Justice's mother continues to pace the living room floor, wringing her hands. Every so often, she approaches the window and draws back the nets to scour the streets. She moves to the phone to check it is still working. She flops down into a chair, frustrated.

Mr Cringe

Act 2, Scene 3

Will the Real Mr Cringe Please Stand Up?

Scene opens on Justice in a dark and gloomy room. He has had a superb time singing and dancing all the way to Mr Cringe's abode and now that they have arrived, the novelty is gradually wearing off. All of a sudden, common sense and a little fear are kicking in.

Mr Cringe: La la la! Welcome, my boy, welcome! Make yourself at home; take the load off your feet. (*He points to an easy chair)*

Justice: Er, actually ... I need to go, 'cause my mum, she'll be so angry with me.

Mr Cringe: Nonsense! How rude would you appear should you leave so soon?
I've not even given you your surprise yet!

Justice: Oh? What surprise is that then?

Mr Cringe: Well, I thought you were keen to leave?

Justice: Well, since there's something going on ... I suppose I can hang on for another five minutes.

Mr Cringe: Oh, yes, Justice, there's definitely something going on ... it would truly be worth hanging on here!
Why don't you make yourself comfortable? I'll just get ready.

Justice: I am comfortable. What do you need to get ready for, then?

Mr Cringe: Well, this surprise, of course!
You said you wanted some fun and excitement in your life, didn't you?
Well, how would you like to feel the feeling of fun and excitement right to the very core of you? Right in your bones?

Justice: How do you mean?

Mr Cringe: I told you I was a jack-of-all-trades, didn't I?
Well, did I mention that in my repertoire it says I'm also a scientist?

Justice: I like science.

Mr Cringe: Oh goody!
Well, I'm about to perform an experiment...

He pushes Justice into the easy chair and flips a switch on its side. It clamps Justice's wrists and ankles into place. Mr Cringe moves to strap his head down.

... on you! Ha ha!

Justice: Hey! Hey, mister! What are you doing?
Let me go! Please let me go.
Help! Help!

Mr Cringe: Hold still, young man. The more you wriggle the tighter it all feels.
Now, no use yelling for help, nobody can hear you in this soundproof room!
Hee hee hee! I've thought of it all!
Tell me, Justice, do people often comment on the size of your mouth?
Ever tell you it would be better off shut?
Well, you've given me a supreme idea for my latest invention and I think you might even grow to like it!
I've got a plan you see! And you are a very important part of it. All I need to do to show the world how great I am is right here! I will finally gain the recognition I've been waiting for. I will be the one to throw science to a new and exciting level and everybody will be after my invention.
Ha ha ho! Oh yes, just lie back and relax, this won't hurt at all!

He begins to whistle the tune to the song Coming Out To Play *(words to be found in Act 3 Scene 4).*

Fade to black.

Act 2, Scene 4

Desperate Measures

At Tata's house: Emmanuel is talking to Tata's parents in their front room. Emmanuel is sitting, holding his mobile, and keeps checking it to make sure he hasn't missed any calls; in the other hand he jingles his keys.

Wallace is standing close and, although he has little respect for this man, he tries to be as empathetic as possible. He passes the TV remote from one hand to the other. Faith sits passively and looks on.

Wallace: So, still no sign? What happens when you call his mobile? Any luck?

Emmanuel: No, It goes straight to voice mail. But knowing Justice, he probably didn't charge it. The man at the corner shop said he hasn't seen Justice all day. Bet if we'd skipped a paper payment, it'd be a different story. Hmph!

Wallace: Well ... hmmm.

Faith: He wouldn't have gone far; he's probably just in a park somewhere.

Emmanuel: You said Tata hadn't seen him?

Wallace: Yes, that's right; he hasn't seen him since school.

Emmanuel: You don't mind if I just have a quick word with him, do you?

Faith: Well ... to be honest I don't see...

Wallace interrupts her abruptly.

Wallace: It can't hurt, although you probably won't learn anything new.
Tata! Tata, come down!

Enter Tata

Wallace: Now, Tata, Justice's dad would like to talk to you about Justice.

Tata: Good evening, sir.

Emmanuel: Hello, Tata. I know you must have heard that Justice was expected home from the corner shop hours ago, but he's not turned up.
His mother and I are very worried now.
Have you seen him or heard from him?
Has he been in touch at all?

Tata: No.

Emmanuel: Where do you think he might have gone?

Tata: I'm not sure.

Emmanuel: But you must have some idea. (*Spoken a little aggressively*)
Think, Tata, please think!

Faith stands up.

Wallace: He said he doesn't know.

Emmanuel: If you hear anything...

Faith: Come, Tata, it's time for bed.

Exit Tata and Faith. Wallace starts to show Emmanuel out.

Wallace: I think it's time to call the police ... it's getting dark now.

Emmanuel: Please call us if he gets in touch.

Wallace: Of course we will.

Act 3, Scene 1

What's That Noise?

Justice is alone, very weak and disillusioned. He's having trouble walking straight, but is trying to make his way home. He still has a little way to go and every now and then he stops to catch his breath. He's hearing voices and feels like he has been drugged. The reality is about to reveal itself.

Act 3, Scene 2

Looking For Justice

Emmanuel is still out looking for his son. Now it is dark and cold and it has started raining. He's on a busy street in the middle of a crowd, it is rush hour. He stops a few people to ask if they have seen his missing boy.

Emmanuel: JUSTICE! JUSTICE! JUSTICE! JUSTICE! WHERE ARE YOU, JUSTICE? JUSTICE! Oh, where is this boy? Oh, God, please let him be all right.

Strangers walk past and he stops them as they pass him, showing them a picture from his wallet; they shake their heads and hurry on.

Emmanuel: Please look. Look at the picture; are you sure? Are you sure you haven't seen him?

More people approach and pass by; he tries again.

Emmanuel: Excuse me, my son is missing, he's only eleven, this is his photo. Have you seen this child? Please! (*He pauses, feeling lost*)

JUSTICE! JUSTICE! Son, where are you?

Act 3, Scene 3

Call in The Professionals

At Justice's house: his mother is talking to two police officers. The female officer (PC 1) is taking note of Justice's particulars whilst the male (PC 2), is talking to Hope, who appears slightly agitated but co-operative. As the discussion progresses, she becomes less calm. She clearly demonstrates her worry and anxiety by wringing her hands and fidgeting.

PC 1: So the last time you saw Justice was around 4pm?

Hope: Yes that's right. I sent him to the local shop.

PC 2: Can you tell us what he was wearing?

Hope: Blue jeans and a red t shirt; he took his jacket, which is black and blue.

PC 2: And footwear?

Hope: Oh. Er, I'm not sure. Probably his trainers. It's so dark now; when are you going to get out there and look?

She raises her voice at this stage, irate that the police are wasting time talking to her and not actively looking for Justice.

She is at the window again.

PC 1: We already have officers out looking for your son, but there's still more information we need from you. Did you have any kind of disagreement with your son before he left?

Hope: No, no ... Nothing like that. Everything was fine and this is not like Justice.

PC 2: So he's never run away before?

Hope: No, never. His dad is still out looking now.

Her tone changes from being quite sure of something to sudden realisation, almost shock, that she will have to live without her child.

Something has happened to my baby, I just know it. Oh God!

PC 1: OK, try not to worry. We have all the information we need for now; we'll be in touch if there's anything else.

They stand to exit and Justice's mother begins to weep uncontrollably. As she is now out of earshot, the police officers begin a private conversation.

PC 1: So, what do you think?

PC 2: She seemed genuine enough. Maybe it's an open-and-shut case.

PC 1: Or maybe there's more to it. She seemed a bit edgy when I asked her if they'd had a row.

PC 2: Nah, I think you're barking up the wrong tree. Let's radio in, find out if anything's turned up yet.

Fade to black.

Act 3, Scene 4

Meet the Dwarves

Justice stops in the 'middle of nowhere'. He looks around, spots a street sign that says 'Middle of Nowhere'. He is in a desolate area on an empty street. He kicks the sign in frustration and yelps out in agony; he hops around holding his foot.

After a short while he stops, he leans against the sign and tries to catch his breath. The voices in his head are getting louder and more audible. (SFX: voice-over of several jumbled voices in various incoherent to highly coherent conversations).

He shakes his head in an effort to lose the sounds, but the voices won't leave him, instead they break into song. (Visuals become foggy and slightly distorted).

Song: *Truly Justified*

Verse 1: We're building our new home, we've only just moved in.
There's plenty of space in our new place, we just can't help but grin!

Chorus: How much is the rent? It's cheap as chips could beeeeee!
How much are the bills? There are hardly any to seeeeeeeee.
How far to the shops? There's no real need to goooooooo,
It's so warm and snug in our brand new hole.

Verse 2: Though we're small, we're truly happy!
What more could we need? We've managed to climb to a spot so sublime.
Yes, we're gonna have a real swell time!
We've waited oh so long, we really could have cried,
But now we're in our palace it's truly justified!

Unison: JUUUUSTIFIIIIIIIIED!

Repeat Chorus

Now the focus switches to Mr Cringe as he leaves his abode with a spring in his step, rubbing his hands together in glee and cackling to himself. He makes his way down the street. He whistles a tune and breaks into song as he comes across a man frantically looking for his son.

Song: ***Coming Out To Play***

Justice, Justice, it's a lovely day;
Justice, Justice, coming out to play?
Put your jacket on, Tell your mum you won't be long.
I'll be waiting 'round the corner, Oh I'll be waiting 'round the corner!

He continues to whistle this tune as he approaches Justice's father, who is trying to get any member of the public to take a look at a picture of his son. Mr Cringe walks past him, circles him and lingers in front of him. Justice's dad is not having any luck with the passer-by and automatically moves onto the next one – Mr Cringe.

Emmanuel: Have you seen my son? This is his picture; please take a look.

Mr Cringe: Your son? (*He peers at the photograph*)

Emmanuel: Yes, do you recognise him? Have a good look. You've seen him, haven't you? You know his face?

Mr Cringe: Well ... he does look a touch familiar.
But no, I don't think so; I must be mistaken.

Emmanuel: What? But you just said he looked familiar. Take another look.
Here's a better picture. Look at this one, it's more recent.

Emmanuel becomes a little more frantic at this stage, but does not suspect anything.

Have a look in the light; please look harder.

Mr Cringe: Nope. Sorry, my old son. I don't know your lad!
But good luck. I hope he turns up without too much bother!

He begins to walk away and Justice's dad loses all hope. He puts his pictures back into his pocket and turns his back to the old man, who begins to sing again ...

Song: Justice! Justice! It's a lovely day.
Justice! Justice! Coming out to play?
Put your jacket on, tell your mum you won't be long.
I'll be waiting 'round the corner, Oh yes, I'll be waiting 'round the corner!

As Justice's name rings out, his father shakes his head in confusion. He turns around slowly as the shady character he has just addressed vanishes into the foggy shadows. Something has just dawned on him. He begins to call after the man.

Emmanuel: Hey! Wait, mister. Hold on, how did you know his name? I hear you singing. I never told you my boy's name! Wait!

Exit Emmanuel in a hurry.

Act 4, Scene 1

Safe But Not Quite Sound

Scene opens on Tata's house: Justice has managed to stagger this far and collapses a few doors away. Tata happens to be looking out of his window and spots a shadow in the darkness. He can't be sure, but the shape could be that of his best friend ... Tata opens his bedroom window and sticks his head out.

Justice manages to make a low groaning sound before passing out. Tata rushes downstairs and out of the house, family in tow. His mother gets on the phone to Justice's household. The scene glows with blue lights and sirens ring out; the ambulance arrives.

Act 4, Scene 2

The Singing Villain

The scene opens on Justice in a hospital bed: he's passing in and out of consciousness. His mum and dad are by his bedside. A nurse is taking his temperature, checking his medical chart, etc. When the nurse leaves, Justice's mum fusses at his hair, smoothes his bedding down and murmurs soothing words. His dad sits in the corner, staring at the floor.

Hope: OK, baby. You're going to be fine. Just fine. He just needs to rest.
Results were all clear. That proves it, doesn't it? Yes-o! My boy is strong.
Just rest, Justice.

Emmanuel: Of course. He's made of tough stuff. I never thought for a minute that ...
I mean, I was sure that he was only around the corner ...
I could just feel it, you know?

Hope: Yes, there was no way my boy would be gone for good.

Emmanuel: It felt like I was searching forever, high and low; it was so dark ...

Hope: Sounds like you want a medal! Don't you know searching is the right thing for a father to do for his lost child?

Emmanuel: A medal? What? No! It's just that I ... what I'm trying to say is ...
I can't believe we've got him back. I felt like I'd searched every street and everywhere and yet nowhere.
I felt like I was waiting for a phone call that was never going to come.
Then when you called to say he was back, well, I can't even describe my feelings.
I was hoping and praying and stopping people in the street...

Hope: I don't want to talk about it.

Emmanuel: But they didn't want to stop or look at his picture...
I guess it was the rain and it was so cold; everyone just wanted to get home. All so miserable. Except this one man ... There was a man that...

Hope: I said I don't want to talk about it.

Emmanuel: But it's just that this stands out, it was really strange...
I remember him ... singing ... and...

Hope: What is wrong with you? Can't you hear me?

Emmanuel: But there is something we need to discuss.
I mean before the police make their own conclusions.
They've given us time, but Justice will still have to file a report.
It was the strangest thing ...

Hope interrupts him again before he can expand.

Hope: Ema, I don't want to hear it. Not now! My baby isn't even conscious yet.
I don't want to think about the why's, how's and who's.
I don't want to think about anything else.
I just want to sit here, with my boy. And pray...

Fade to black.

Act 5, Scene 1

Hold the Fort Tata!

ONE WEEK LATER

School has resumed and the scene opens on a classroom. Mrs Alexander has her back to the class whilst she makes notes on the board. She speaks aloud as she does so, making reference to some literature on her desk every now and then. Of course, the class takes this opportunity to whisper and/or pass notes. One boy leans across another in order to effectively whisper to Tata.

Marcus: Oi, Tata! Tata?

Tata turns his head away from his work to look at Marcus.

I heard that Justice has gone nuts! That's why he's not at school.

Another boy takes the opportunity to add his opinion to the conversation.

Second Boy: Yeah! I heard that he's loopy, man! He's got voices going round his head!

The boy throws some balled-up paper in Tata's direction, hitting the back of his head. He stifles a laugh. Tata begins to show signs of getting upset: fists clench, mouth tightens, etc.

Tata: The only one loopy round here is you! Idiot!

At that moment Mrs Alexander notices the attention of her pupils is diverted, but she only hears Tata.

Mrs Alexander: Oh really, Tata! So, you have the answers to the literacy test you're going to sit next week do you? Is that why you think it's OK to talk during lessons?

Tata: No, Mrs Alexander.

Mrs Alexander: Is your memory so short that you've forgotten that you are on your very last warning?

Tata says nothing, but throws an angry glance at the boys who were teasing his best friend. He is aware that Justice is the talk of the school, but he refuses to allow the bullies to get the better of his best friend's absence.

Second Boy: (*In a whisper*) Your mum's an idiot!
(*The boy throws a paper-clip at Tata but misses*)

Tata: You just wait!
(*Another exchange of angry glances occurs as the scene ends*)

Act 5, Scene 2

Bud among the Taste Buds

Justice is at home with his mum fussing over him, which, secretly he is enjoying. He is feeling more himself, although he has not been outside since being discharged from the hospital some days ago. He is upstairs in his bedroom, looking in the mirror, opening and closing his mouth and speaking in between each action.

Justice: OK, people. I know you're in there. (*He opens his mouth wide to take a look.*)

I saw you last night when I was brushing my teeth. (*He opens wide again.*)

Who are you? Show yourselves. Come out so that we can talk about this.
I promise not to bite.

He pauses, then notices a slight movement by his lower left pre-molar. A dwarf emerges and gingerly steps forward. Justice gasps and the dwarf falls back as a result of that action. He dusts himself off and begins to speak in rhyme. Note that at this point, the effigy should take centre stage.

Bud: What's the meaning of life? I hear you say, Is it to work or is it to play?
Scoping out the friend or foe, hunting high and creeping low.

How tricky to be this small, so tiny am I so close to the floor.
But now we have this brand new home, we work and play, all over we roam.
Who are we? Friend or foe? Why friend, of course! Don't you know?
I know it's mighty odd to see.

A dozen men among your teeth!
But we balance the acid in your mouth.

And we keep everything neat in our house.
We're the best neighbour you could need, Quiet as mice, oh yes indeed!

Justice: Excuse me! Hi.

Bud: Yes?

Justice: Who exactly are you and what are you doing in my mouth?

Bud: (*Breaks into song*) I am His Excellency's representative, Bud.
His Excellency is Chief Tong. He is head of all the dwarves in our fair land.

Justice: Bud? Your name is Bud? Well, what are you doing in my mouth?

Bud: We reside in your mouth.

Justice: How did you get there and why do you sing everything?

Bud: We are here on a programme and we sing for a living!
It's in our nature to be giving.

Justice: Well, how about giving me a break!
Look, I still don't quite get this whole you living in my mouth thing, but I think it would be best if you told the main man to come out.

Bud: Ho Ho! You wish to see the chief? You wish to see the chief?
You must book a meeting if you want to see the chief.

Justice: Book a meeting with my own mouth?

Bud: It might be quicker if I speak with you; you'll get all you need if you hear me through!

Justice: OK, Bud, look. I'm not as happy as you are with your crew living in my mouth.
Nobody asked me before they moved in.
I mean, what happens when I eat and when I want some peace and quiet or privacy?

Bud: Justice, what's the problem?
Relax. Just take five and sit back.
We can't leave now; it took so long to unpack.
Mr Cringe put us here and now we've settled in.
We feel right at home; it feels like we're ...

(*Justice interrupts.*)

Justice: Aaaagggh! Stop the singing!
Can't you just talk normally! And who put you here?

Bud: Just give it a chance and then you'll see all the possibilities.
What an advantage to have us living with you: the fun is endless, you haven't a clue! He's an inventor you see, and it doesn't end with me!
There are quite a few of us and there are more on the way,
Mr Cringe is really something of a genius, wouldn't you say?
We have a real purpose, living here with you
Like I said the fun is endless – you haven't a clue!

Justice: Aaahhhhh! What possibilities?
You're not living WITH me, you're living IN me!

At that point Justice's bedroom door opens unexpectedly: it's his mum. At this stage the effigy should be out of sight; either lights down on that part of the stage or the effigy should exit.

Hope: Justice? Who are you shouting at?

Justice: Hunh?

Hope: I heard you shouting.

Justice: Oh. No, er ... I was, errr ... rapping.
Yeah! I was looking in the mirror and rapping to myself.
(*He begins to demonstrate dancing and rapping in the mirror*)
Yeah! You're not living in me, you live with me and if you don't leave,
I'll need some money!
What? What?!!! Yeah!

Hope: OK, OK, I get it. Well, that's enough. If you've finished up here come down and lie on the couch. I've made you Tomato soup and I want to give you your medication.

Justice: OK, mum, I'll be right down.

Exit Hope.

Justice moves closer to the mirror, but there's nothing there.

Justice: OK, little man. Bud. Where are you? She's gone.
I want to know who put you here.
You not coming out? OK, but we'll have to talk about this.

Exit Justice to the sitting room.

Act 5, Scene 3

Justice Comes Clean

Hope hands Justice a tray with food and medication in it.

Hope: Let me know when you've finished that soup.
I'll come and collect your bowl.

Justice: OK, mum, thanks.
Oh, by the way, Tata wants to come over after school.

Hope: Are you sure you're feeling up to having people over?
I mean, you don't want to over-exert yourself.
It's so soon. You've only been out of hospital two minutes!

Justice: Awww, mum! Please? I really want Tata to come over. It's been ages.

Hope: Yeah, and you know why!

Justice: But I just thought that ... oh! (*Justice looks almost close to tears*)

Hope: OK. He can visit and I'll make something special for dinner.

Justice: Yesssssss! Thanks, mum, you're the best.

Hope: Mmmmmhmmmm! Close your mouth.

She smiles at Justice and squeezes his face affectionately, which makes him wince in pain.

Justice: Ouch!

Hope: Oh, sorry, baby. Still a bit sore?

Justice: Only a little bit.

Hope: You know, Justice, whenever you're ready to talk to me about that whole ...episode, I'll be here and I think you know how worried we were about you. Me AND your dad?

Justice: I know. And I AM sorry, mum. And I will tell you. It's just that I can't remember everything. Stuff keeps coming back to me in bits.

Hope: Well, the doctors did say it might take a little while for the flashbacks to get into order.

Justice: Mum, there is something that I remember.

Hope: What?

Justice: Well, that night I went missing, I wasn't actually kidnapped like I told the police...

Hope: How do you mean?

Justice: Well, you know I told the police someone kidnapped me?

Hope: Yes, I know that. Get to the point.

Justice: Well ... (*Justice is interrupted by the phone ringing)*

Hope: Go on...

Justice: Aren't you going to get that?

Hope: It's not important.

Justice: It might be! I'll be right here!!

Hope tuts, and reluctantly moves to answer the phone. She's back in seconds.

Hope: It was the school. They just wanted to check how you're doing.

Justice: More like, when I'm coming back. More like, if I'm really sick!

Hope: More like, as you were saying?

Justice: What was I saying?

Hope: Justice! Don't play games!
You said you were not kidnapped but you told the police that you were.

Justice: Yeah. I remember voluntarily going to this place. I was OK going there.
I can't remember being dragged there or anything.

Hope: But the doctors found traces of a drug in your body which would have made you unaware anyway. Are you sure?

Justice: Yeah. I remember singing.

Hope: Singing?

Justice: Yes... on the way to this place. We sang.

Hope: Who's we?

Justice: The man and I. We sang all the way there; that's how I know he didn't force me to go.

Hope: What did he look like? This is very important.

Justice: I can't remember.

Hope: Try your best. Think.
The police need a description so that this madman can be caught.
You don't want him to try this again, do you?

Justice: You don't think he'll come after me, do you?

Hope: What! No way! I didn't mean after you. God forbid.
No. I meant you don't want him to come after another little boy, do you?

Justice: Like who? You mean Tata?

Hope: Justice, no! Look, I just want you to help the police as much as possible, that's all.
I mean, I don't understand why you would follow a complete stranger anywhere.
I've always warned you about trusting people. It just doesn't make any sense. You wouldn't just go off with someone, would you, Justice?

Justice: Mum, I'm feeling a bit tired now.

Hope: Oh, OK, baby. You can finish your soup later. Relax, take a nap.

She removes the bowl, adjusts the cushion behind his head and lets him snuggle down on the couch. She watches him with a worried expression on her face.

Tata and Justice

Much later... Enter Tata.

Justice: Hi, Tata!

Tata: Wasssupppp? Wow, man! Feels like ages!

Justice: I know! How's school?

Tata: School? It's alright I guess...

Tata takes a seat and continues in a more serious tone.

Look, what's the deal? What happened to you that night?

Justice: Aaahhhhh, man! It's not all clear.
You know, things are still a bit foggy in my head.

Tata: Yeah, course. But you must remember something?
Do you remember ending up outside my house?

Justice: Yeah, I remember seeing your ugly mug staring back at me!
Ha! Thanks for that.

Tata: It was nothing. It's not the only time I've saved your skin lately, either.

Justice: What do you mean?

Tata: I had a bit of a fight after school today.
Lucky for me no teachers were about, otherwise who knows what Mrs Alexander would do.

Justice: Tell me about it! So who was the fight with?

Tata: That idiot Marcus.

Justice: Oh, I can't stand him, he's so dumb! I hope you taught him a lesson!

Tata: Course! But before I could finish, some seniors came along and split us up. Anyway, the point is that it all started because he was going on about how crazy you are.

Justice: What?

Tata: Well, what do you expect?
The whole school is talking about how you've lost your marbles.

Justice: Well I haven't!

Tata: So what happened then?

Justice: I can't believe it!

Tata: Unless you set the story straight, this is just gonna go on and on until something more interesting happens.

Justice: But how did they find out anything? What did you say?

Tata: Me? Nothing!

Justice: So, how does anybody know anything then?

Tata: How would I know? I'm the one fighting your battles and defending you and you're accusing me of being the big mouth.
I don't know why I even bother.
Getting my butt kicked because of you and you ain't even told me the full story.
For all I know you might just be crazy anyway!

Justice: Thanks, thanks a lot! That's obviously what you really think.

Tata: (*almost shouting*) Well, why won't you explain then?

Justice: Because I can't remember!

Tata: Well, when you do, let me know! (*He gets up to leave*)

Justice: Where you going?

Tata: Home.

Justice: OK, OK, don't go. I'll tell you what I can remember.

Tata: You better!

Justice: Sit down then. (*Tata sits down*)
I thought you said you taught Marcus a lesson?

Tata stands up quickly and grabs his bag to leave in a hurry

Alright! Alright! Sorry. Wait! Sit down. (*Tata sits*)
I...I hear things. Sometimes, it's ... er ... Oh, it doesn't matter.

Tata: What do you hear?

Justice: I'm not crazy.

Tata: I know that.

Justice: It's like singing. Lots of singing in my head, but it's not me singing.
It's more than one voice; it's so hard to explain.
You won't get it unless you see it; nobody will.

Tata: Singing? What kind of songs?

Justice: Oh, I don't know! Nothing we would listen to anyway.
It's just that this singing is not coming from inside my head, as in, it's not coming from inside my mind.
If you follow? It's as if the voices are inside my body.
And they are actually inside my head.

Last night, when I was taking my bath, the singing started up.
At first, I ignored it and it started to get louder, so I started singing myself, out loud.
Anyway, it went on and on, and I thought 'when is this going to end?'

Tata: So, when did it?

Justice: Not for ages. Anyway, after I tried to out-sing this ...

Tata: Choir?

Justice: Choir. I got out of the bath to brush my teeth.
And you know when you're looking in the mirror brushing?
I thought I caught a glimpse of something racing across my mouth.

Tata: (*Starts laughing and can't stop*) You mean your toothbrush?!!!

Justice: Shut up! Oi! OK, forget it. I'm not saying another word.

Tata: (*Tries to control himself*) OK, no! I'm sorry. I'm serious now, see?

Justice: Anyway, I took a closer look and it's really difficult to explain; you won't believe it, but ... I've got little people living in my mouth.

Tata: What?

Justice: It's true.

Tata: What? What are you on about?

Justice: I knew you wouldn't believe me. But I've seen them and spoken to one!

Tata: You've got PEOPLE living in your gob????

Justice: Keep your voice down. My mum doesn't know.

Tata: Like she's gonna believe me if I tell her!
Justice, I think those painkillers the doc gave you are too strong.
They're making you see things. Or you're imagining things.
The pills are making you see stuff, I think.
When did you last take your medicine anyway?

Justice: It's not the medicine. I know what I saw.

Tata: So, how come I can't see them now then?

(*At this stage he's peering towards Justice's mouth, but is not able to see much at all*)

Justice: Because, you lemon, they're not singing at the moment.
They only appear visible when they're singing.
And I don't know why, but they do.

Tata: OK.

Justice: OK, what?

Tata: Nothing. Just OK. What time was your last dose? How many did you take?

Justice: You don't believe me, do you?

Tata: Not really, no. I need proof to believe it's not the drugs talking!

Justice: Whatever. To be honest, The Choir started singing that night I went off with that man, when I was trying to make my way home. So it can't be the pills.

Tata: Ummmm. I bet that dude has planted one of those tracking chip thingies on you, and it's picking up somebody's radio, and you're getting the feedback from that, yeah! Now that's a reasonable explanation!

Justice: That would make more sense, but then what would explain the little man I saw?

Tata: The one running around your mouth?

Justice: Yeah.

Tata: Illusion?

Justice: No! I told you. I think that man planted The Choir in my mouth.

Tata: But why?

Justice: I don't know ... yet.

They pause for thought with puzzled looks on their faces.

Tata: So, when they start singing, will I hear them?

Justice: How would I know????

Tata: I don't know! Do you still feel ill then, or are you feeling any better?

Justice: I feel OK.

Tata: OK enough to play Time Lapse*?

Justice: OK enough to kick your butt on Time Lapse!

Tata has brought his computer game over and proceeds to connect it up to the TV. Before long, the boys are having a fantastic time.

Justice: And I win, again! Ha-ha!

Tata: Just because I let you. How bad would I feel if I kicked the butt of a sick boy?

Justice: Yeah, right! Want another go?

Tata: Nah.

Justice: Someone's tired of losing.

Tata: Justice, are you really alright?
I mean, really.

After a long pause

Justice: Anyway ...

Tata: So, why haven't you told your mum yet then?

Justice: Because, whilst I was trying to drown the singing out, I started thinking about what my mum does for me.
She works so hard, two jobs and everything. My dad is such a waste- man!
He doesn't help out at all!
I've heard them arguing, and my mum is always saying how he's ...

Scene fades into mimed argument between Justice's parents, Hope and Emmanuel.

Hope: ... Such a bad husband. You don't give me anything.
You don't DO anything; all you do is take, take, take!
I'm so tired of you and your lazy attitude!

They go back into a mimed argument and Justice continues his conversation with Tata, unaware of the minor interruption.

Justice: Anyway, I thought, although I'm too young to work, how could I help my mum?
And then I thought there must be a way for me to make money from this situation ... that would make my mum happy!

Tata: You mean this little man in your mouth?

Justice: And the rest!
Don't you think people will pay to see something as strange as that?

Tata: Maybe ...

Justice: Maybe?

Tata: But, Justice ...

Justice: Think about it, Tata!
We could charge people to have conversations with my mouth and I wouldn't have to say a word!
At first I was so freaked out by the whole thing, but then I had a conversation with one of them earlier

today and later got to thinking about something he said.
The possibilities, I just have to give them a chance.

Tata: Hunh?!! Justice ... I don't know where you're going with this.
Wouldn't it be better to tell your mum so that you can see a doctor?
Anyway, how come the doctors didn't pick up on this if there are people in your mouth or whatever?

Justice: I didn't tell them!
Anyway, I think the little guys must have been hiding or something.

Tata: Yeah, OK!

Justice: Tata, come on! We could make soooo much money from this!
I'll make you my promoter. You can arrange the events and find me gigs!
We can go to the papers, they'll pay!

Tata: You mean, you want me to tell people to give us their money to talk to mini-people living in your mouth?
People I can't even see? People I'm not sure actually exist?

Justice: Are you saying you don't believe me?

Tata: Well, what do you expect?
Who actually knows what happened that night you went missing?
The police? Your mum? The doctors? I certainly don't.
You say I'm your best friend, but I feel like I don't even know you right now.

Justice: Why didn't you just say it's a bad idea?

Tata: That's what I've been trying to say for the past how long? Century!

Justice: Well, I think it's a cool idea.

Tata: You always think your ideas are cool and then you end up getting us both into trouble!

Justice: Well, you never complained before!

Tata: Well, it never involved a kidnapping before, or some kind of crazy man.
I mean, how do you know he won't try it again?
Considering you haven't told the police who he is.

Justice: That's because I don't know who he is.

Tata: Even if you did. The point is you didn't see how worried your dad was.

He came to my house, you know.
Your parents thought I might have known where you went; normally best friends do.

Justice: Not in a kidnapping.

Tata: Well, was you kidnapped or not?

Justice: Kinda. Well, not exactly.

Tata: Oh, I give up. You can't even tell me the truth about that; I certainly don't believe you about 'The Choir.'

Justice: Look. There's still a lot I can't remember.
The doctors said I was drugged and that would affect my memory for a little while.

But what I do remember is that I was with this guy and I followed him to this place and when I got there, I felt like ... a bit ... well, it was really creepy.

Anyway, I had forgotten all about the milk my mum sent me out for in the first place, so I remember telling the guy I had to leave, but then something happened.

I can't remember what, but I do remember having a really bad headache when I woke up.
I was so drowsy and then I felt OK.

I remember getting a bit lost on my way home and then I felt drowsy again and that's when all the singing started.

That's the truth, Tata.

Tata: Really?

Justice: Really.

Tata: Wow. To be honest, I can't see what you're talking about and I don't want to tell people about something I've never seen. So now what?

Justice: All I really want is to do something nice for my mum. Don't you understand?

There's a long contemplative pause. Then Tata smiles widely at his old friend and gives him a friendly punch on the arm.

Tata: Of course I do! So what's the plan?

Justice: First things first. I've got to ... oh! ... (*Justice pauses, listening*)

Tata: Got to what? Justice? Are you OK?

Justice holds up a finger, signalling Tata to wait a minute.

Tata: (*Under his breath*) What's going on now?

Justice: Do you hear it?

Tata: Hear what?

Justice: Look!

Justice opens his mouth wide and Bud appears with The Choir humming in the background. The effigy enters and occupies centre stage.

Tata: Oh my! What in the name of all that is sane?
Justice, they're there, they're really there!

Justice tries to speak without closing his mouth.

Justice: I told you! And you thought I was making it all up!

Tata: Shush! Don't try to talk! They're walking around.
Oh, Justice! Did you know they've got furniture set up here!

Hahahaha! It's like a doll's house. This really is something.
This is real!
Hello? Hi!

Tata tries to put his hand in Justice's mouth in an attempt to touch the dwarves and they swerve to avoid contact.

Justice: Hey! Don't do that!

Tata: I just want to know what they're made of.

Justice: By putting your hand in my mouth? Nasty!

Tata: Looks like you've got dirtier things in there than my hand!
If they're real as in not made of plastic, that means they must use the toilet.
So have you got a toilet in your mouth or ...

Both: Ugggghh!

Tata: Wow, I can't actually believe it. I mean,
I thought you might have been playing around ...
they're soooo tiny!
Open up again ... I promise I won't touch!

Fade to black.

Tata, Mr Cringe and The Dwarves

Act 5, Scene 4

By George, Fancy That!

Scene opens on Emmanuel in the local bookies, placing a bet.

George: No more bets, thank you.

SFX: a loud voice-over comes on, commentating on a horse race. The reaction of the crowd is fully charged and the shop becomes rowdy. It's a smoky atmosphere and Emmanuel is right at the centre of the action.

There are lots of random shouts of 'Come on!' and 'Yes!' 'That's it, my son! Move, move!' and other such remarks. The commentator announces the winning horse and there are whoops and cheers as well as sounds of disappointment.

Emmanuel tears up his ticket in frustration and throws it down. He looks around ... pushes through the crowd to the front and at the cash desk ...

Emmanuel: George, George. Sticky Toffee came in last, again.

George: I know. I saw.

Emmanuel: George, you know I put my last tenner on that.

George: Look, I can't help you today. You chose your luck.

Emmanuel: Oh, George, please! My Missus is gonna be so angry with me.

George: I can't give you your money back. (*In a hushed tone*) What do you think my boss will say if the books don't balance two days in a row?

Emmanuel: George, I'll owe you one. I just thought it was a sure thing.
I could have sworn that horse was gonna come first.

George: Well it didn't, did it? You lost and you'll just have to get over it.
That's it, there's nothing I can do. Next please! Oh, morning, boss.

*At that moment Mr Cringe walks in, whistling his new trademark tune (*Coming Out To Play*). He walks around the counter towards the back room and doesn't notice Emmanuel ... but Emmanuel notices him. Mr Cringe nods in George's direction.*

Mr Cringe: Everything OK, George?

George: Yeah, fine.

Mr Cringe exits into the back room. At this stage, Emmanuel has completely forgotten about his lost bet and is in shock that this criminal is the manager at his local bookies. He stands there, lost in thought for a minute or two.

He approaches the counter again and tries to get George's attention. George is in the middle of counting out a customer's winnings and tries to ignore him until he's finished.

Emmanuel: George. George?

George: That's ten, twenty, thirty, forty ...

Emmanuel: George, I just need to ask you something.

George: Eighty, ninety, one ...

Emmanuel: It's not about money!

George: What then?

Emmanuel: Your boss? That man, he is your boss, right?

George: Cringe? Yeah.

Emmanuel: Cringe, that's his real name?

George: Yeah, Miles Cringe. Why? Do you want to see him?

Emmanuel: NO! I ... does he live round here?

George: Yeah, he lives down near the heath. What's going on?

Emmanuel: Oh ... er ... nothing. I just thought I knew him, that's all.
But I don't, so never mind. I'll see you later.

Exit Emmanuel.

Act 6, Scene 1

Another Unsuspecting Individual

Scene opens on Mr Cringe in his back room. He is sitting at his desk with his feet upon it. He has a Dictaphone, on which he records his report in a low and even tone.

Mr Cringe: Eagerly anticipating the next few days when I will be able to switch on the device planted inside the unsuspecting individual.

At present he is probably still in the hospital as my reliable little spies informed me he had been checked in shortly after the incident.
Everything went according to plan on the night and the unsuspecting individual was a perfect guinea pig for the upgraded version of this bug.

Hee heee! The mini-kingdom should be flourishing and the experiment is no doubt going smoothly. The dwarves are the perfect size, the right quantity and yes…this time I shan't fail.
The original unsuspecting individual is required back at headquarters in precisely three days for routine testing. Another unsuspecting individual is required for future experiments and I will...

Mr Cringe is interrupted by a knock on the door. He abruptly switches off his Dictaphone and throws it into a drawer, which he promptly locks. He straightens himself out before responding.

Mr Cringe: Yes?

George: Mr Cringe, sorry to disturb you. I just wanted to check if you need anything.
I'm going over to the bank shortly.

Mr Cringe: Erm, actually, George, I don't think so. Many thanks.

Exit George.

Mr Cringe: Hmmmm. George, perhaps? No, too close for comfort.
Somebody I cannot be linked to. But who?

Fade to black.

Act 6, Scene 2

Back to Being the Sidekick

Tata and Justice are in their school playground.

Justice: Roll up! Roll up! Come and see wonders you could never have imagined!
£5 for a chat, special discount for today only!

Tata: Come over, take a look! Sights here you'd never believe!

Marcus and his side-kick walk over to where the boys are standing.

Marcus: Oh look! It's dumb and even dumber!
What are you lot shouting about anyway?

Justice: Move on, Marcus; there's nothing for you here.

Marcus: I could say the same thing to you since this is my patch.

Side-kick: Yeah! That's right!

Tata: Here we go!

Marcus: You got something to say about that?

Justice: Yeah, since when has the school playground been 'your patch?'

Tata: Exactly! I don't see your name on it anywhere.

Marcus: Like I need my name on it! You two freaks have been here long enough to know I run the show around here; what I say goes.
If I say it's my patch, you need to move on – fast!

Side-kick: Yeah!

Tata looks at Justice and begins to move on, but Justice drags him back.

Justice: We're not going anywhere. We've got as much right to be here as anyone. Mind your business and kindly move on!

Justice and Tata turn their backs and continue with their banter, encouraging potential punters to stop.

Justice: Come and see a mystery; special prices for today only!

Tata: Come and have a conversation you never thought possible!

Marcus: Hang on! I don't think you get it! Unless I give you the OK, you can't stay.

Side-kick: You can't stay!

Marcus and the side-kick high-five each other.

Tata: Maybe we'll give you a discount if you leave us alone.

Justice: Tata!

Tata: Well, if it'll get him to go; money's money anyway!

Marcus: Give you lot my money? What would I do that for?

Justice: Nah, don't worry about it. Tata made a mistake.

Marcus: What you selling?

Justice: Nothing to you!

Tata: It's a conversation unlike any other.

Justice: Tata!

Tata: With mini-people.

Justice: Shut up will you!

Marcus: What? Oh, I get it; so you really are crazy, and now you've gone cuckoo too!

Side-kick: Cuckoo! Cuckoo!

Tata: Nobody's cuckoo. Pay a fiver and you'll see for yourself.

Marcus: You're on my turf and now you wanna charge me for it?
I've got an idea; how about you show me what you're doing to rip everybody off before I kick your heads in?

Justice: You think we're afraid of you?

Marcus: I know you're afraid of me, you rubber-lipped plonker!

Justice: I know you've been talking about me and spreading rumours, but it doesn't even matter. You hear me? I don't care.
It doesn't matter what bullies like you say.
Calling me names and acting like you own the place!

Marcus: Here we go! Loopy's lost it again!

Justice: You've got issues, Marcus. I don't know what they are, but you won't solve them trying to take them out on me.

The bell rings to indicate an end to break time and everybody starts to leave the playground.

Tata: Now that was telling him! It really is good to have you back. Nobody handles Marcus like you can, not even me! We better get moving. I don't need a detention.

Justice: Let's go.

Tata and Justice move swiftly ahead of Marcus and his side-kick, who stands shaking his head at Marcus and holding back a snigger.

Marcus: What you laughing at, you joke!

Tata: So much for this being a money-making plan.

Justice: How much did we make?

Tata: Not much; a fiver.

Justice: Is that it?

Tata: That's it.

Justice: Well, once word spreads that will all change.

Tata: Hmmmm.

Justice: Well, anyway, we need to make sure we're out on time so that we can skip ahead of the crowd after school.

Then hopefully we'll gain some interest on the main road.

They head into class.

Act 6, Scene 3

Seek and You Shall Find

Scene opens at the local library with Emmanuel tapping away on a computer keyboard. He murmurs aloud to himself every so often.

Emmanuel: OK, let's do a search ... Cringe ... Miles ... enter.

SFX: librarian's voice: "The library will be closing in 10 minutes. Please bring any items to the front desk."

Emmanuel: Ah! Come on, come on! This thing is too slow! Right, Miles Cringe. Manchester? No. New York, No! Bristol, No. So many here ... come on, London. OK. South London, Bermondsey. Miles Cringe, Miles Cringe ... Cringe. Ah hah!
"July 12th 1989: Miles Cringe, of Bermondsey, South London, was today arrested for kidnapping a nine-year-old boy from the area, whom he held for a total of 16 days."
Er, excuse me? How do I print this?

Act 6, Scene 4

Strike Two

Justice and Tata are heading home from school; they have run ahead of the crowd in order to draw in more attention from the passing school flock. Simultaneously, Mr Cringe is creeping along the other side of the stage, acting suspiciously and peeping in through the bushes, watching the two friends, etc.

Justice: OK! I know you've all been wondering what the fuss in the playground's all about; well, now's your chance to find out!
Step over here and cast your eyes on wonders that will amaze!

Tata: That's right, you'll never know anything like it; roll up!

The crowd hustles past and continues to ignore them. The crowd is so large and rowdy that Tata soon gets 'swallowed up' by the mass and nobody even notices when Mr Cringe reaches in from the bushes and grabs Tata. His hand is over Tata's mouth.

The crowd continues to shout at Justice to move out of the way and they continue to move past without interest. Eventually the crowd subsides and the only person left behind is Justice. He looks behind and around him, confused.

Justice: Tata? Tata? Where are you? Tata? Tata!

He races after the crowd ahead to see if Tata is there. But to no avail. As he runs ahead, Mr Cringe drags Tata off stage in the opposite direction.

Act 6, Scene 5

The Police Station

Emmanuel is at the reception desk of the local police station.

Emmanuel: Excuse me, I've been waiting to see somebody for the past 30 minutes now!

Receptionist: Someone will be with you shortly, sir.

Emmanuel: Am I next?

Receptionist: Yes, you are.

Emmanuel's mobile phone starts ringing.

Emmanuel: Hello? Oh, Justice. How are you? What? No, your mother should be at work; she's working double-shift tonight.

What's the matter? Why would I have any idea where Tata is?
I'm in the police station.

No, of course I've not been arrested!
I'm making an inquiry into the man that took you.
I've found some-

Emmanuel is interrupted by a Police Officer calling.

PC: Mr, er, Mr um ...? Right, who's next, please?

Emmanuel: I'm next! Justice, I have to go, I'll call you back. (*He ends the call*)
Yes, I've been waiting here for over an hour now. I'm next, please!

Act 6, Scene 6

Typical!

Justice is at home, in his school uniform, and is looking at the house phone. He is clearly very upset and pulls the phone out of the wall and throws it across the room. He begins to abuse his father loudly.

Justice: Typical! Why would I call him anyway? He's so unreliable.
Obviously, this is something I'll have to handle myself.

He leaves the room angrily.

Act 7, Scene 1

The Crazy Scientist Strikes Again

Mr Cringe is bundling an unconscious Tata out of his car and into his laboratory, undetected. He sings to the tune of Coming Out To Play *as he does so.*

Song: Tata, Tata, what a funny name! Tata, Tata, come and play my game!
I've got a cunning plan, For experiments I'm your man.
You'll enjoy this when it's over, Yes, you'll enjoy this when it's over!

Inside the dark lab (only one spotlight) Mr Cringe gently lowers Tata into the same chair he used for Justice and secures him into it.

And when you wake up, my dear, we'll have a little bit of fun.
Hee hee hee, ho!!!

Exit Mr Cringe.

Meanwhile, Justice is looking for Tata everywhere he can think of. Finally, he decides to see if he has gone home. He approaches Tata's house and knocks. The door is answered by Tata's brother.

Chico: Yeah?

Justice: Oh, hi, Chico.

Chico: Yeah?

Justice: Er ... Is Tata home?

Chico: Don't you two normally walk home together?

Justice: Sometimes. Ummmmm, not always.

Chico: So, where is he then?

Justice: So, he's not home yet?

Chico: What do you think? No, he's not!
Hang on a minute, look at the time! It's starting to get dark.

Justice: OK, then I better be off. Laters.

Chico: I said, 'Hang on a minute!'

Justice freezes.

Chico: What's going on? You're acting a bit shifty.

Justice: Dunno what you mean.

Chico: I mean, you're acting a bit shifty.

Justice: No.

Chico: And I think you're up to something, but you're not letting on...

Justice: No!

Chico: What are you up to? Where's Tata?

Justice: It's not me. And I don't know where he is. I ... I, I was with him after school and then all of a sudden he just vanished. I've been looking everywhere.

Chico: Vanished? To where?

Justice: I don't know.

Chico: Well, why didn't you say something earlier?
You been standing here with your mouth open, looking like a right lemon and lying your backside off when all along you're up to your usual bag of tricks!

Justice: But I don't know anything. I'm not up to anything I swear.
I don't know what's going on; that's why I came here, 'cause I thought Tata might have just come home.

Chico: Yeah, right; so why did you lie and try to walk off?

He goes inside to reach for his jacket.

Justice: Because I was trying to do the right thing and still I got the blame.

They begin to jog down the street.

Chico: What do you expect? Where did you see him last?

Chico takes his phone out of his pocket and tries Tata's mobile number.

Justice: Uhhh, outside school; we started walking home together and got caught in the crowd. The next thing I know, he's gone.

Chico: Think, Justice! Where in the world could he be? Tata doesn't just go off without a word; he's not like you!

Justice: Hey!

Chico: Get thinking! Where did you go?

Justice: I can't remember exactly...

Chico: His phone's going to voice mail. Let me try my mum.

Justice: No! Don't call her. She'll only blame me.

Chico: What? Is that all you can think about? I always knew you were selfish, but this is something else! Tata is supposed to be your best friend; you say you've looked everywhere for him and if that really is true, you should be worrying about him, not yourself. When are you going to grow up, Justice?

He begins to dial his mother from his mobile.

Act 7, Scene 2

Busted!

In Mr Cringe's laboratory, Tata wakes up, startled and confused.

Tata: Help!!! Help me! Hello? Somebody?

Enter Mr Cringe.

Mr Cringe: Oh! Ho ho ho! He's up! Hello, my dear! Nice nap?

Tata: Who are you?

Mr Cringe: I'm your chum; you remember me, don't you?

Tata: I remember you snatching me in the street. What do you want with me?
If it's money, I'm sure my family will give it to you.
Just let me go, OK?

Mr Cringe: Hmmmmm? Oh, money, hey? I wish it were as straightforward as that.
But that's not what I want. No, I want more than that. I don't need your money! What I need is your compliance, and I've already got that, thanks to my chair. Money, a very interesting offer! How much do you think you're worth, Tata?

Tata: How do you know my name?

Mr Cringe: Well, I'm good friends with your good friend, Justice, I believe?

Tata: (*Makes an audible gasp*) Oh my God!
You? You took Justice?

Mr Cringe: Hardly! Hahaha! Oh no! Justice came here of his own free will.
That's right, free as a bird he was!
And we had some serious fun, he and I! Just like we will now.

Mr Cringe stands over Tata with a very scary-looking device attached to a syringe.

Tata: I, I, I already knew that anyway. Justice said he followed you.

Mr Cringe: Oh he did, did he? Well at least he's not a liar. No, he's just very naive!

Tata: What do you mean?

Mr Cringe: I mean that he is the easiest case yet!

Tata: So you make a habit of pulling kids off the street, hunh?

Mr Cringe: I didn't have to pull Justice! Ho ho! Like I said, he was the easiest yet!

Tata: Why are you doing this mister ... mister er ...? What is your name?

Mr Cringe: You can call me Mr Cringe; after all, I think this should be one of many regular meetings ... I intend for us to be very good acquaintances!

Tata: Why? Wh ... wha ... What you gonna do?

Mr Cringe: Well, since you ask ... I intend to demonstrate how an ordinary boy like you can house a whole team of dwarf-sized...

Tata: Oh no! No way! I don't want people in my mouth!

Mr Cringe: Oh, then it's a good thing I'm not putting anything into your mouth, isn't it? Once I've sedated you, I'll be delivering a special dose of 'Dwarf City'
... into your ear!

Want to know what comes next?
Well, after the well-developed implementation of the Pseudoachondroplasiamentosis Farm* into your ear, during which you'll feel a tingling sensation all over, you'll then begin to feel slightly light-headed.

This feeling will promptly be followed by what we, of the scientific world, call benign positional vertigo, which means you'll get a bit giddy!

After four to six minutes of constant jabber from the voices within, you'll get more accustomed to the company of your new friends, which I will review after 7 to 10 days of maturity.

Tata: What? Uh, but Mr Cringe, sir, look, you don't really want to do this; what's the point in all this? You already have something going on with Justice.

Those dwarf things in his mouth, you know; what's the point in doing this to me? Please!

Mr Cringe: Ah! So he told you all about his experience with the delicate implementation of Pseudoachondroplasiamentosis, did he?

Tata: The implementation of what?

Mr Cringe ... The implant!

Tata: Oh! Yes, and I think it's something that needs to be shut down.
You can't just go round planting things inside people.

Mr Cringe: Things? Things! Is that what you think my multi-purpose farms of dwarf-sized implementations are? How wrong you are!

They are the epitome of what the future represents.
A new generation of technological know-how!
The best part? Only I know how!! Hahaha!

You wait, my boy; those plants, they'll be called for by the FBI, the CIA, the most intimate kind of mole you can get and the most reliable kind of bug in this modern age.

There's so much profit to be made and a great deal of fame to be claimed … by me of course.
This will be a turning point in the world of science and, most importantly, in the life of Miles E. Cringe!
(He pauses, lost in thought)

Yes, and so! The show just must go on, my dear. Just lie back and relax! I want to say you won't feel a thing, but I think that would set us off on the wrong foot, so I'll just say ...

Mr Cringe is interrupted by a serious disturbance. SFX: loud shouts and the sound of smashing glass, as his window comes crashing in. Enter Justice, followed closely by Chico.

Tata: Justice?

Justice: Tata, you OK? What you doing to my best friend?

Mr Cringe: Why it's Justice and ...

Tata: Chico? Is that you?

Chico: Get away from my brother, you freak!

Mr Cringe: Justice! You and your friend are just in time for the party!
And look, there's plenty of my special 'potion' to go around!

Justice: I don't think so, not this time!

Tata and Chico move towards Mr Cringe with the intention of disarming him.

Mr Cringe: Ooooh, impressive, Justice.
I like this new-found personality; bravado, if you will!

Justice: You won't get away with this. You need to drop the thing and let Tata go.

Mr Cringe: What I need are even more volunteers, and I think you two have just stepped up, hahaha!

Cringe flicks a switch and suddenly a cage falls from above their heads, entrapping them.

Justice: Hey! Hey!

Chico: Oi! What do you think you're doing? Let us out! Let us out now!
I'll get you for this; you won't get away with all this!

Mr Cringe: Oh yeah? Who's going to stop me now?

A team of armed police hurriedly enter.

Police: STOP! STOP! ARMED POLICE, DON'T MOVE! DON'T MOVE!

PC 1: DROP THE WEAPON, NOW!

Mr Cringe: OK, officer, it's OK. I'm putting it down.
No need to panic; it's state of the art and I'm putting it down slowly.
Don't shoot. No need to panic.

PC 2: DOWN ON YOUR KNEES, NOW!

Mr Cringe: That's a valuable instrument, that is, not a weapon.

Enter Emmanuel.

Emmanuel: Justice! Justice! Where's my son?

Justice: Dad! Dad! It's OK. I'm in here.

Emmanuel: Tata! You're alright, you're both alright. Thank God!

Justice and Chico are released from the cage by police officers. Chico runs to the side of his brother and tries to release him. Justice runs to his father. Meanwhile, an officer begins to disarm and cuff Mr Cringe.

PC 1: MILES CRINGE, YOU'RE UNDER ARREST FOR ONE COUNT OF KIDNAPPING AND SEVERAL COUNTS OF ...

Cringe begins to shout over the sound of the officer's voice.

Cringe: I'll return; you've not seen the last of me, not by a long chalk, oh no!
I'll be back!

Justice: Oh, Dad, am I glad to see you!

Chico: Yeah! Your timing was perfect.

Emmanuel: How could you two be so stupid as to try and tackle this by yourselves?
Chico, I expected more from you.

Chico: I tried to call mum but there was no answer, and dad's at work.

Justice: Dad, I just wanted to do right by Tata. We thought we would be alright.
I guess we underestimated the whole thing.

Tata: But, was I glad to see you, because a minute later and I would have had it!

Emmanuel: That would never have happened.

Justice: But it could have and it would have been all my fault.

Tata: What are you talking about?

Justice: I should have just told the police everything at the very start, then none of this would have happened.

Emmanuel: Son, it wasn't your fault; you couldn't remember.

Justice: Dad, I wasn't totally honest with you and mum.
I wasn't kidnapped and, although I really couldn't remember this laboratory until today when the pressure was on, I knew what this guy was capable of.

I nearly couldn't find this place and then I saw the 'Middle of Nowhere' street sign and knew you couldn't have been too far.

I should have been more responsible, less selfish; I know that now.
I should have been there for Tata and I'm sorry I let you down.

Tata: Well, you remembered this place when it mattered the most; that's the main thing. I just want to get home.

Chico: Me too!

PC 3: Gents, we'll need you to come with us to make official statements.
There'll be a medic along to check you over shortly.

Fade to black.

The following day, Tata and Justice are at Justice's house in the sitting room.

Tata: What a crazy night.

Justice: Tell me about it. I couldn't sleep last night. My head was just spinning.

Tata: Yeah, I had trouble switching off too. I don't think anyone in my house slept.
I could hear my parents talking 'til all hours.

My mum doesn't want me hanging with you anymore, but I think my brother's been talking her round.

A bit strange considering I always thought Chico didn't like you!

Justice: Me too. I'll have to work on her myself.
I've been thinking about something Chico said to me last night.

I know I've been a bit dumb and I should probably have just thought more about the consequences of my actions, because when I think what could have ... I mean, when I consider ... what I'm trying to say is, if anything had happened to you I just ...

Tata: Hey man. It's cool. We're cool, yeah?

Justice: Yeah. Yeah.

Tata: But I've got a question. What you gonna do about Bud and the rest of The Choir?

Justice: I told my folks about it all.

Tata: What? You did?

Justice: Yeah, I thought it would be best to come clean; there's no point in hiding it from them.

It will all come out if we have to go to court anyway, so my mum's booking an appointment with a specialist to have them removed.

Tata: Wow!

Justice: Yeah. I never thought I would say this, but I'm actually gonna miss those guys.

Tata: You did the right thing, man; you did the right thing. I bet your mum didn't realise your dad was trying to crack this case already,did she?

Lights fade to spotlight on Justice alone as he delivers his monologue to the audience.

Justice: No! Nobody did. I have to say that I was kind of impressed too and it's kind of nice to get a bit of attention from him, even though it started from something so crazy. I realise now I underestimated that crazy man, Cringe.

Nothing is ever what it seems. I should never have trusted him and it was a mistake to keep The Choir and try to make money out of it.

Most importantly, I'm so glad for a solid friendship like the one I have with Tata. I just keep thinking about what could have happened ...

Light dims on Justice and spotlight comes up on Hope and Emmanuel in an embrace on a different part of the stage.

Hope: I know I've been hard on you lately, and I want you to know I value what you did for Justice ... and Tata. I think I under-estimated you and ...
(*Emmanuel interrupts her by putting his finger to her lips.*)

Emmanuel: You and I and Justice are a family; you're going to see a lot of change around here. Starting with me.

Lights dim and the spotlight is lifted on police officers raiding the laboratory. SFX: Mr Cringe's voice-over plays as they work, rifling through papers and files.

Mr Cringe: The one that got away. There's always one that gets away.
However, this is only the beginning; they don't know how much further I can go.

Underestimate me, will they? I had plans; no, I still have plans.
They'll see, they'll all see! (*He raises his voice*)

I have only just started; you hear me?
Let me make my phone call! Let me make my call, do you hear?

Police Officer: Sarge, you better come and look at this.
Looks like evidence of previous cases.

Fade to black.

Spotlight comes up on Mr Cringe in prison overalls on the phone.

Mr Cringe: Operator, I need to be connected directly to a Mr C. E. Cringe; that's right, Charles Eli Cringe.

Seconds pass before the connection is made and then ...

Hello, Charlie boy? It's daddy ... it's time for you to step up to the plate, son. I need you.

THE END

Time Lapse
The latest computer game played by Justice and Tata

Pseudoachondroplasiamentosis Farm
(Pronounced su-do-akon-dro-plaseeah-mentosis)
A team of dwarf sized individuals with a genetic autosomal disorder

Justice is My Name

Salihah Agbaje ♩ = 100 Daisy Watkins

2

5
Cl.
Tr. Solo
take aw - ay my side - kick and my fav - ourite game As no mat - ter what the time, ex
Pno.
Vc.

8
Cl.
Tr. Solo
cite - ment is my name! As far as it goes, it's dif - fi - cult to see Me
Pno.
Vc.

11
Cl.
Tr. Solo
in the same place as bore - dom may ev - er be I am
Pno.
Vc.

13
Cl.
Tr. Solo
al - ways at the end where fun is run - ning mad, With Ta - ta and me ar - ound, you'll
Pno.
Vc.

16
Cl.
Tr. Solo
on - ly ever be glad! Yeah, Jus - tice is my name and ex - cite - ment is my game Wher
Pno.
Vc.

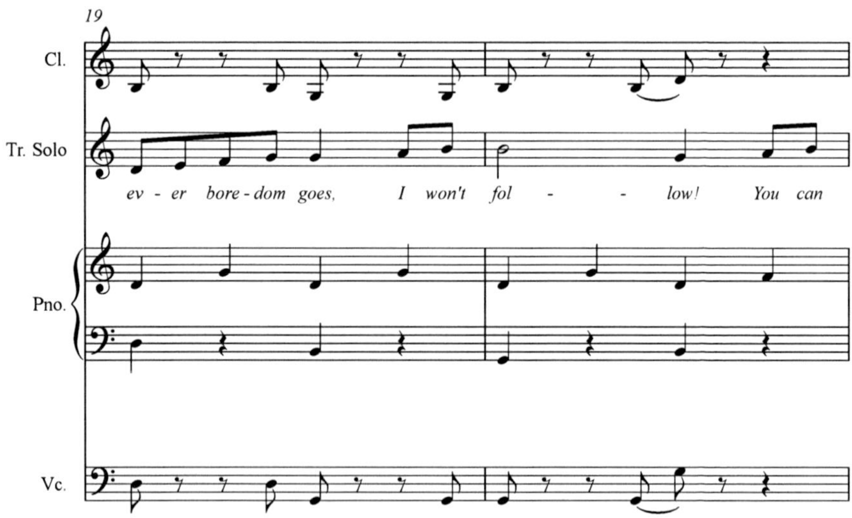
19
Cl.
Tr. Solo
ev - er bore - dom goes, I won't fol - - low! You can
Pno.
Vc.

21
Cl.
Tr. Solo
take aw - ay my side - kick and my fav - ourite game As no
Pno.
Vc.

23
Cl.
Tr. Solo
mat - ter what the time, ex - cite - ment is my name!
Pno.
Vc.

Follow Me

Salihah Agbaje ♩= 100 Daisy Watkins

2
8
Cl.
Bar. Solo
Pno.
Vc.
p
won - der - ful thing a - bout me you see, is all the ver - sa - ti - li
11
ty. I of - fer this, and I of - fer that. I've

3
14
Cl.
Bar. Solo
Pno.
Vc.
cresc . . .
sp
more than two fea - thers in me cap!
Ho - cus po - cus and
sp
sp
cresc . . .
sp
17
simile
Cl.
Bar. Solo
Pno.
Vc.
zip - pa - di - doo,
I'm some - thing di - ffer - ent,
simile

4

19
Cl.
Bar. Solo
Pno.
Vc.
p cresc . . .
cresc . . .
some - thing new, I'm some - thing rare and don't you know, this
p cresc . . .
p cresc . . .
p cresc . . .

22
Cl.
Bar. Solo
Pno.
Vc.
mf
f
mag - ic stuff is not for show! It's real you see _ and
mf
mf
mf

25
Cl.
Bar. Solo
whats - more, I'm sure of how to dou - ble the score.
Pno.
pesante
f
pesante
Vc.
f

28
Cl.
tr
f
Bar. Solo
Bring - ing fun and joy ar - ound When bore - dom was all that
Pno.
f
f
Vc.
f

6

Cl.
Bar. Solo
could be found. Yes, the won - der - ful thing a - bout me you see, is
Pno.
Vc.

Cl.
Bar. Solo
all the ver - sa - ti - li - ty, I of - fer this and I of - fer
Pno.
Vc.

37
Cl.
Bar. Solo
Pno.
Vc.
dim . . .
that, I've more than two or three fea - thers in me cap!
dim . . .
dim . . .
dim . . .

40
Cl.
Bar. Solo
Pno.
Vc.
p
mf
Mag - i - cal worlds are in my hands, Come close my boy, And I'll
p
p
p

43
Cl.
Bar. Solo
show you lands, Be - yond your wild - est dreams and more This
Pno.
Vc.

46
solo
Cl.
cresc . . .
mf
cresc . . .
Bar. Solo
kind of stuff you've not seen be - fore!
Pno.
mf
mf
cresc . . .
mf
Vc.
cresc . . .
mf

9
49
Cl.
cresc . . .
f
Bar. Solo
Pno.
cresc . . .
f
cresc . . .
f
Vc.
cresc . . .
f

52
Cl.
f
Bar. Solo
f
Yes, the
Pno.
f
f
Vc.
f

56
Cl.
Bar. Solo
won - der - ful thing a - bout me you see, is all the ver - sa - ti - li
Pno.
Vc.

59
Cl.
Bar. Solo
ty, I of - fer this and I of - fer that, I've more than
Pno.
Vc.

62
Cl.
Bar. Solo
Pno.
Vc.
mf
mf
two or three fea - thers in me cap! Jus - tice what's your de
mp
mp
mp

65
simile
Cl.
Bar. Solo
Pno.
Vc.
sire? Mo - ney? Fame? Or climb - ing higher?

68
Cl.
Bar. Solo
I can make your life more in - te - rest - ing shall we say?
Pno.
Vc.

70
Cl.
Bar. Solo
Fol - low me to some - where more priv - ate and we'll play. Are you
Pno.
Vc.

72
Cl.
Bar. Solo
rea - dy to ex - per - i - ence some - thing new and sur - real? You'll
Pno.
Vc.

74
Cl.
cresc . . .
f
Bar. Solo
cresc . . .
f
on - ly get this once chance so don't go and blow it, how do you feel?
Pno.
cresc . . .
mf
cresc . . .
f
Vc.
cresc . . .
f

77
Cl.
Bar. Solo
How do you feel? Af - ter some exc - ite - ment?
Pno.
Vc.

79
Cl.
Bar. Solo
Af - ter some - thing new? Well come on then, boy You know what to do!
Pno.
Vc.

82
Cl.
Bar. Solo
Let's have some fun, fol - low me, come al - ong En - joy - ing your -
Pno.
Vc.

85
Cl.
Bar. Solo
self just can't be wrong. Yes, the won - der - ful thing a -
Pno.
Vc.

16

89
Cl.
Bar. Solo
bout me you see, is all the ver - sa - ti - li - ty, I of - fer
Pno.
Vc.

92
Cl.
Bar. Solo
this and I of - fer that, I've more than two or three fea - thers in me
Pno.
Vc.

95
Cl.
Bar. Solo
cap! Yes, the won-der-ful thing a - bout me you see, is
Pno.
Vc.

98
Cl.
Bar. Solo
all the ver-sa-ti-li - ty, I of-fer this and I of-fer
Pno.
Vc.

18

101
Cl.
Bar. Solo
that, I've more than two or three fea thers in me cap!
Pno.
Vc.

Truly Justified

Salihah Agbaje

♩ = 100

Daisy Watkins

2

6
Cl.
cresc
f
Tr. Solo
cresc
f
We just can't help but grin! How much is the rent? It's
Pno.
cresc
cresc
f
Vc.
arco
cresc
f

9
Cl.
Tr. Solo
cheap as chips could beee! How much are the bills? There're
Pno.
Vc.

11
Cl.
Tr. Solo
har - dly any to see. How far to the shops? There's no real need to go, It's
Pno.
Vc.

14
Cl.
mf
Tr. Solo
so warm and snug in our brand new hole. Though we're
Pno.
mf
mf
Vc.
mf

17
Cl.
Tr. Solo
small we're tru - ly hap - py! What more could we need? We've
Pno.
pizz
Vc.

19
Cl.
Tr. Solo
man - aged to climb to a spot so sub lime Yes we're gon - na have a
Pno.
Vc.

22
Cl.
Tr. Solo
real swell time! We've wai - ted oh so long, we real - ly could have cried But
Pno.
Vc.

25
Cl.
cresc
Tr. Solo
now we're in our pal - ace it's tru - ly jus - ti - fied! Justified!
Pno.
cresc
cresc
Vc.
cresc

28
Cl.
Tr. Solo
How much is the rent? It's cheap as chips could beee! How much
Pno.
arco
Vc.

31
Cl.
Tr. Solo
are the bills? There're hard - ly any to see. How far
Pno.
Vc.

33
Cl.
Tr. Solo
to the shops? There's no real need to go, It's so warm and
Pno.
Vc.
35
Cl.
Tr. Solo
snug in our brand new hole.
Pno.
Vc.

Coming Out to Play

Salihah Agbaje

Daisy Watkins

8
Cl.
Tr. Solo
I'll be waiting 'round the corner
Pno.
Vc.

10
Cl.
Tr. Solo
I'll be waiting 'round the corner
Pno.
Vc.

About The Author

Salihah Agbaje is an actress, television presenter and drama tutor. She has always loved writing and started off as a youngster writing poetry and performing it for private audiences.

A lively and avid performer onstage and off, she holds a BA Degree in Media Performance from the University of Luton.

Mouth Almighty is Salihah's first published work. It has gained popularity touring around South London schools and libraries as a small scale production.

Salihah lives in London with her family and is currently writing another piece for children. She can be contacted at the email address below:

Salihah@mouth-almighty.com

Lightning Source UK Ltd.
Milton Keynes UK
UKOW050727170412

190885UK00001B/1/P

9 780956 586100